L. FRANK BAUM'S

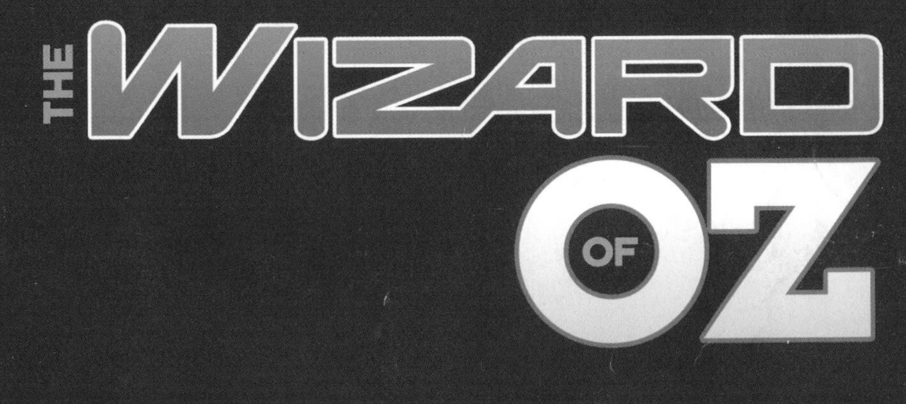

STONE ARCH BOOKS
MINNEAPOLIS SAN DIEGO

L. FRANK BAUM'S

THE WIZARD OF OZ

RETOLD BY MARTIN POWELL

ILLUSTRATED BY JORGE BREAK

COLORED BY BENNY FUENTES

DESIGNER: BOB LENTZ
EDITOR: DONALD LEMKE
ASSOC. EDITOR: SEAN TULIEN
ART DIRECTOR: BOB LENTZ
CREATIVE DIRECTOR: HEATHER KINDSETH
EDITORIAL DIRECTOR: MICHAEL DAHL

Graphic Revolve is published by Stone Arch Books 151 Good Counsel Drive, P.O. Box 669 Mankato, Minnesota 56002 www.stonearchbooks.com

Library of Congress Cataloging-in-Publication Data
Powell, Martin.
The Wizard of Oz / by L.F. Baum ; retold by Martin Powell ; illustrated by Jorge Break.
p. cm. -- (Graphic revolve)
ISBN 978-1-4342-1582-6 (library binding) -- ISBN 978-1-4342-1737-0 (pbk.)
1. Graphic novels. [1. Graphic novels. 2. Fantasy.] I. Break, Jorge, ill. II. Baum, L. Frank (Lyman Frank), 1856-1919. Wizard of Oz. III. Title.
PZ7.7.P69Wi 2010
741.5'973--dc22
2009013685

Summary: One day, a cyclone suddenly sweeps across the Kansas sky. A young girl named Dorothy and her dog, Toto, are carried up into the terrible storm. Far, far away, they crash down in a strange land called Oz. To return home, Dorothy must travel to the Emerald City and meet the all-powerful Wizard of Oz.

Printed in the United States of America

CONTENTS

THE WICKED WITCH
OF THE WEST

SCARECROW

THE GOOD WITCH OF THE NORTH
TIN MAN
DOROTHY
TOTO

CHAPTER 1
THE CYCLONE
On the gray Kansas prairie, a young girl named Dorothy lived with her Aunt Em and Uncle Henry.
Not a single tree grew in the dusty soil, which stretched to the bleak sky in all directions.
Yet young Dorothy was often filled with laughter, especially while playing with her little dog, Toto.
You want me to throw it again? You're funny, Toto!
Uh-oh, Toto! This game's over!
Looks like it's going to rain!

Toto! Wait!

Everybody into the storm cellar!

Em! We've got to get to shelter!
Where's Dorothy?!
I can't see her!
Dorothy!
Where are you, girl?
Toto! Where are you, Toto?
There you are, boy. Come on, quick! It's a bad storm, Toto!
We have to get down into the —
Oh!

The great cyclone raised Dorothy's little house higher and higher, carrying it away.

It was dark and windy, but Dorothy remained brave and held little Toto close to her.

Then, as quickly as it began, the howling stopped. A sudden shock made the girl catch her breath.

Their house was safely on the ground again.

This doesn't look like Kansas, Toto.

MUNCHKIN LAND

Welcome to the Land of Oz!
You have killed the Wicked Witch of the East and freed our people!
Look for yourself, child!
Who was she?
The Witch of the East. She has controlled the Munchkins for many years.
You have saved them all, Dorothy!

Who are the Munchkins? And who are you?
The Munchkins are the little people who live in this land of the East. And I am the Good Witch of the North.
You're a witch? I thought all witches were wicked!
There were only two evil witches in the Land of Oz, and one of them is gone forever.
But her sister, the Witch of the West, is far more dangerous.
The sooner you go back home, the safer you'll be, my child.
But how? Toto and I don't know how to get back home!
Why not ask the great Wizard of Oz?
The Wizard of Oz? Is he good or is he wicked?
The Great and Powerful Oz is good, and he is mightier than the Witch of the West.
He will send you home.

Oh! They are shrinking to fit my feet!
Never take them off. These Silver Slippers have great magic power.
How will I get to the Emerald City?
It is a long walk to the Emerald City, where the mighty Oz rules . . .
Now that the Witch of the East is dead, you should have her Silver Slippers.
The way to Oz is simple enough . . .

CHAPTER 3
THE JOURNEY TO THE GREAT OZ
Just stay on the Yellow Brick Road, and all will be well!
Thank you so much, Good Witch. I wish you could go with me.
I cannot do that, but I can give you my magic kiss which will protect you.
Don't be afraid, my child.
Very soon the Wonderful Wizard of Oz will send you home.

Dorothy and Toto set off on their adventure . . .
Soon . . .
Good day.
Did you speak?

I certainly did speak. How do you do?
Well, we're doing fine, thank you. And you?
Not well at all. It's boring being perched on a pole all day and all night.
Yes, you must be very uncomfortable. Let me help you down.
Thank you! Thank you very much! I feel like a new man!

I'm Dorothy from Kansas. Toto and I are going to the Emerald City to ask the Wizard of Oz to send us back home.
Do you think the wizard might give me some brains?
Most of the time it's not so bad being a Scarecrow.
But how am I ever to know anything without brains?
Then come with us. I'll ask Oz to do all he can for you.
You will? Oh, thank you!

Toto and I will be happy to have you join us.
Don't worry, he never bites.
Oh, I'm not afraid of Toto. I'm not afraid of anything . . .
. . . except, of course . . .
. . . a lighted match!

Miles and miles later . . .
Do you want a bite of my apple?
No, thank you. My mouth is only painted on.
If I cut a hole in it so I could eat, the straw would all fall out.
Well, *my* mouth is as dry as straw. Let's try to find some water.
Of course, I don't know anything, but maybe we shouldn't leave the Yellow Brick Road.
Maybe you're right, Scarecrow. These woods are quite dark and scary.
Don't worry, Dorothy. I'll lead the way.
What is that?!
How would I know? I've never seen anything like it.

It's a man made of tin! And I think I hear him breathing!
Are you all right, Tin Man?

I was caught in the rain while chopping down that tree. I've been rusted solid ever since.

This oil can must be yours. Maybe this will help.

Let me oil your arms . . .

Oh, joy!

Thank you! You have certainly saved my life!

We're on our way to the Emerald City, to see the Wizard of Oz.
That sounds exciting! Why do you wish to see the Wizard?
I want the Wizard to send me and Toto back home to Kansas.
And the Scarecrow wants some brains put in his head.
Brains, huh? They aren't the best things in the world, you know.
What do you mean? What's better than brains?
I would ask the Wizard for a heart. Do you think he might give me one?
I don't see why not. Come with us, and we'll ask him.
How do you know you'll like having a heart when you get one?

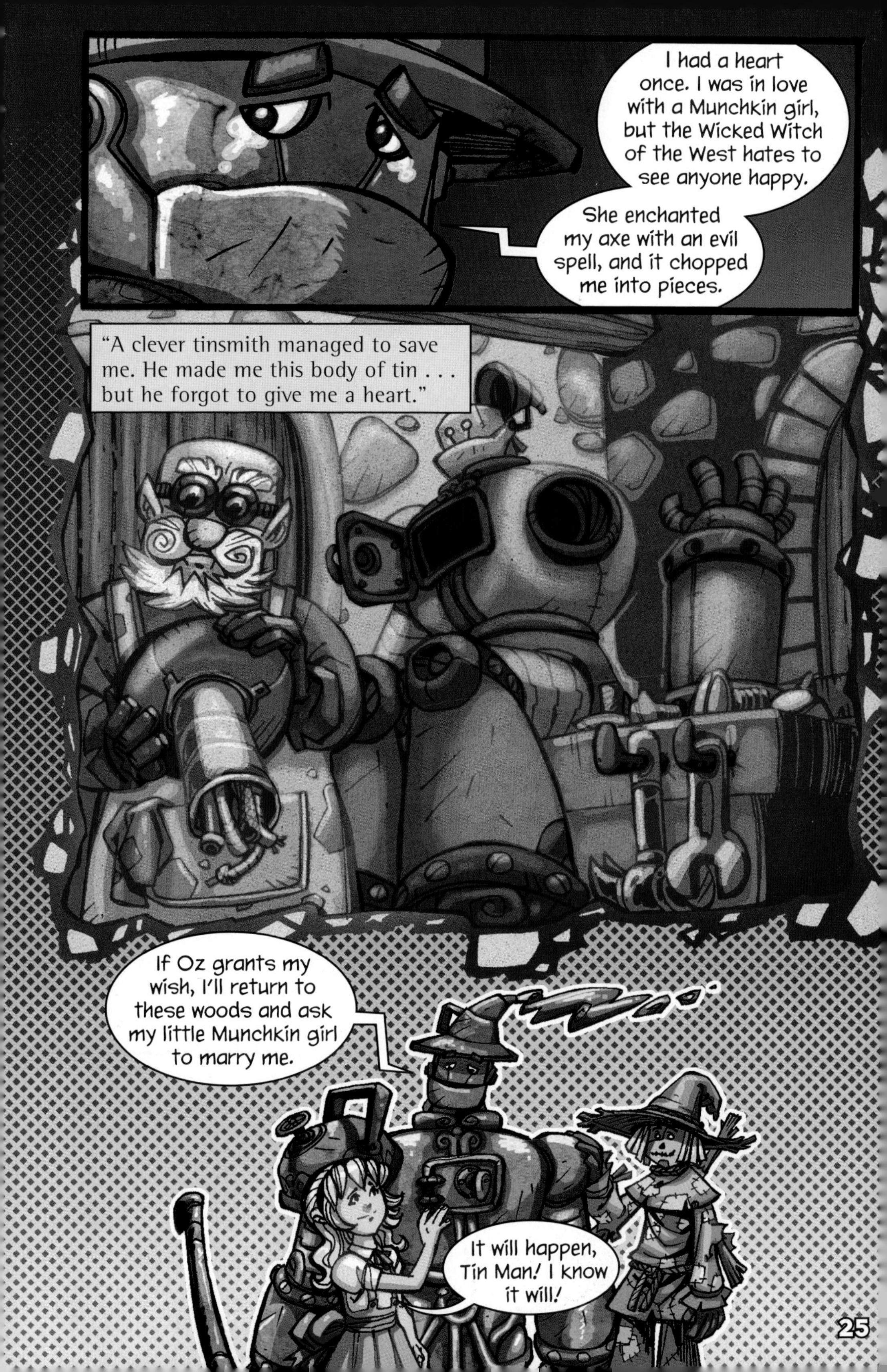

I had a heart once. I was in love with a Munchkin girl, but the Wicked Witch of the West hates to see anyone happy.

She enchanted my axe with an evil spell, and it chopped me into pieces.

"A clever tinsmith managed to save me. He made me this body of tin . . . but he forgot to give me a heart."

If Oz grants my wish, I'll return to these woods and ask my little Munchkin girl to marry me.

It will happen, Tin Man! I know it will!

Dorothy and her new friends kept traveling after the sun had set . . .
How long until we are out of the forest?
Don't worry. As long as I have my axe, I'll protect us all!
Besides, the Good Witch protected you with her kiss.
Nothing can harm you.
GRRRRRRRRR
Did you hear that?!
Something's behind the trees!
There it is again!
I hear it too!
GGRRRRRRRR

GGRRRR!!!
SMACK!!
Toto!!
Don't you dare bite Toto!
You ought to be ashamed of yourself for picking on a poor little dog!
Why, you're nothing but a big coward!
You're right. I am a coward. I should be the King of Beasts, but I have no courage.
I think we should help him.
If we took the Lion with us, the Wizard might even give him some courage.
That's a great idea!

What good friends. I don't know what to say.
That's easy. Say yes! Right, Toto?
BARK!
Let's be off then!
I hope morning comes soon. I'm afraid of the dark.

Meanwhile . . .
THERE'S MORE TO FEAR THAN THE DARK, MY NAIVE TRAVELERS.
MUCH, MUCH MORE.
HAHAHAHAHA!

The next morning . . .
SNIFF
SNIFF
SNIFF
All of you, climb on my back! Now!
Lion, what's wrong?
The Kalidahs are hunting us! They're ferocious monsters!
If we are caught, they'll have us for breakfast!
ROARRRR!
Hang on!

RRRAAAAWWWR!!!
Great job, Lion! That was a close one!
I'll say it was! If I had a heart, it would've skipped a beat!
When they turned around . . .
Flowers! Aren't they beautiful?
I've always liked flowers, too. They're so pretty and delicate and not scary at all.

So, where do we go from here?
We should hurry and get back to the Yellow Brick Road.
Oh, no! What happened to them?
Since I don't have any brains, I can't be sure . . .
. . . but I have heard of a field of poppies. The smell of these flowers is killing them!
This is terrible! What are we going to do?
May we be of service, good sir?

I am the Queen of the Field Mice.
How can we help you?
Your Majesty, our friends' lives are in danger! Can you help us save them?
The Lion is much too heavy to move! This is truly heart-breaking!
Yes, but with the help of the field mice, there just might be a way.
Bring your axe, Tin Man. We need to build something special for this occasion.
After a great deal of hard work . . .
Just imagine how clever I'll be after the Wizard gives me some brains!
Amazing! It works like a charm!

Dorothy? Wake up, Dorothy. Open your eyes and look where we are!
Oh, my!
CHAPTER 4
THE WONDERFUL CITY OF OZ
The Emerald City!

I feel like I've been asleep forever! Am I still dreaming?
I couldn't say! I never dream because I don't ever sleep!
At least you'll never have nightmares like I do!
Soon you will have nothing but good dreams, Lion.
BZZZZZ
Why do you come to the Emerald City?
I'm Dorothy, and these are my friends. We're here to see the Great Wizard of Oz!
Very well, you may enter.
I hope you haven't come here on a foolish errand. The Great Oz might become very angry!

Never take off these glasses! The brilliance of the Emerald City might blind you.
Now follow me . . . at your own risk!
Uh, maybe this isn't such a good idea.
I'll be b-brave for you, Dorothy.
Don't worry, Lion. We're all in this together.
These strangers demand to see the Great and Powerful Wizard of Oz!
More of a polite request, actually, if you please, sir.

Make yourselves at home. I will tell the Great Oz that you are here.
It must be lonely for the Wizard, since he never has visitors.
I was rusting away all alone for the longest time.
I know what that's like.
The Great Oz will see you now.
We're all a bit nervous. None of us have ever seen a real wizard before!
No one has ever seen him. I speak to him through a screen in front of his throne.

Then why did he agree to see us?
I told him about the Silver Slippers upon your feet.
It's not too late to turn back. Are you sure that you want to look upon the face of the mighty Wizard of Oz?
Yes, of course! We have come a very long way to see him.

I AM OZ, THE GREAT AND TERRIBLE!
Who are you, and why do you seek me?!
I am Dorothy, the Small and Meek. We've come to you for help.

How did you get the Silver Slippers of the Wicked Witch of the East?
The Good Witch gave them to me after my house fell on the Wicked Witch.
The mark upon your forehead is also from the Good Witch of the North.
You are very wise! She sent me to you for help.
What do you wish me to do?
Please send me back home to Kansas, where my Aunt Em and Uncle Henry live!

I come for some brains, since my head is stuffed with straw!
I pray that you will give me a heart so that I may once again feel love!
I am a cowardly lion, I come to you for c-courage, so I may finally become K-King of Beasts!
Your wishes shall be granted . . .
. . . but first, you must kill the Wicked Witch of the West!
But we don't want to kill anyone.
When this last Evil Witch is dead, I will make your wishes come true.
NOW GO!

CHAPTER 5
SEARCH FOR THE WICKED WITCH
At the castle of the Wicked Witch of the West . . .
THERE YOU ARE, MY PRETTY LITTLE THING!
The soldier said all we need to do is think of the Wicked Witch, and she'll find us.
That will be easy. I can't stop worrying about her!
Oh, no! A storm is coming!
It's worse than that! Look!
Run! The Wicked Witch has found us!

RRRIP!!
We cannot harm this girl. She wears the mark of the Good Witch!
Then we must take her with us!

Soon . . .
WELCOME, DOROTHY OF KANSAS.
I'M SURE YOU KNOW WHO I AM, AND THE TERRIBLE THINGS I CAN DO.
NOW GIVE ME THOSE SILVER SLIPPERS, OR ELSE!
No! You can't have them!
And I wear the mark of the Good Witch, so you can't hurt me!
BARK BARK!
Dorothy was right. The Wicked Witch could not hurt her.
Instead, the evil woman used her magic . . .

. . . to make Dorothy simply slip and fall.
Ah!
FOOLISH GIRL! DID YOU THINK YOU COULD STAND IN MY WAY?
My slipper!
Dorothy did the only thing she could think of to stop the Witch.
SPLOOOOSH!
NOOOOOOo!!

WHAT HAVE YOU DONE TO ME!?
She's melted!
WOOOSH!!
AHHHHHHH!
SSSSSSSSSS
Who would have guessed that water would be the end of her?

Just as her sister had commanded the Munchkins, the Wicked Witch of the West had ruled the Winkies.
The Wicked Witch's spell has been broken!
You are no longer her slaves!
We're free!

To show their gratitude, the Winkies gave gifts to Dorothy and her friends.
Hurray for Dorothy and her friends! They freed us from the Wicked Witch!
A gold collar! How kingly!
BARK!
How wonderful! A silver oil can!

The Winkies sewed Scarecrow back together again and gave him a walking stick.
Thank you, my friends. I will no longer stumble as I travel.
Look at what I found in the Wicked Witch's cupboard.
I shall give this helmet to the Wizard to prove that the Witch is truly gone.

CHAPTER 6

DISCOVERY OF OZ

Don't touch that! Go away!
BARK BARK!
RRRIP!!
You're nothing but a fake!
It's true. I fooled everyone for so long, but you were too clever for me.
But why?
Years ago, I was a balloonist in a faraway land.
One day, a storm carried me away in my balloon.
When I landed in the Emerald City, the people believed I was a wizard!
After learning about the Wicked Witches, I told the people that I *was* a wizard.
It gave them something good to believe in.

You're a fraud!
Yes, I am a fraud, my friend.
Even so, I think I can help you.
You're going to give me some brains?
In a way. Stuff these pins into your straw head, and you'll feel sharper in no time.
No need to be so sad, my sensitive friend. This should fill your empty chest.
Thank you. I shall never forget your kindness.

As for you, your Majesty, one sip of this and courage will always be inside you!
COURAGE
Oh, joy! I promise to rule with kindness and bravery!
Thank you for helping them, Oz. They are good friends and deserve good things.
Get a good night's sleep tonight, Dorothy. Because tomorrow . . .
. . . we're both going home!

The next morning . . .
I am going to visit my wizard brother who lives far away in the clouds!
While I am gone, Scarecrow will rule in my place!
He is very wise!
Toto! This is no time to play! The Wizard is taking us back home!
MEEOW!
BARK BARK!

BLOOP!
Oh, my! The rope has come loose!
Hurry, Dorothy, or the balloon will fly away without you!
I'm caught in the wind! Good-bye, my dear!
Don't worry, Dorothy. I didn't think of it before, but maybe the Good Witch can help you.
Of course! She could take Dorothy and Toto home!
Oh, can it be true?

CHAPTER 7
THERE'S NO PLACE LIKE HOME
Later, many miles south of the Emerald City . . .
There's only one road that leads south! We'll just keep walking until we get there!
That seems like a long trip.
Aunt Em and Uncle Henry must be worried sick about me by now.
Well, maybe the writing on the Wicked Witch's Golden Cap can unlock its magic!
I think you're right, Scarecrow.
Those pins and needles have certainly made you sharp!
"Eppe, peppe, kakke! Hi-lo, hollo, hello! Zizzy, zuzzy, zik!"

EE-EEE!!
OOO-OOO!!
AAH-AAA!!
We must obey the wearer of the Cap. What is your command, mistress?
Carry us to Glinda the Good Witch, please!

I am Glinda, the Good Witch of the South. I have been waiting for you.
Can you really send me home to Kansas?
Your Silver Slippers have wonderful powers. They can carry you to any place in the blink of an eye.

I'm so happy I can go home, but I don't want to leave you all!
It's okay, Dorothy. We understand.
Your family must be worried sick about you.
Don't worry, Dorothy. I'll protect the Scarecrow and the Tin Man.
Thanks to you, I know what friendship means.
Please don't cry, Tin Man. You'll rust again.
Are you ready to go home, Dorothy?

All right, I'm ready.
Close your eyes, dear. Then tap your heels three times, and make your wish!
KLIK KLIK KLIK!
Take me home!

Goodness gracious!
Did it work, Toto?
The color had returned to Aunt Em's cheeks. And Uncle Henry, who had never smiled, now laughed until he cried.
My darling child! Where in the world did you come from?
From the Land of Oz! And Toto was there, too!
Oh, Aunt Em! I'm so glad to be home!

TALES OF OZ

Considered by many to be the first American fairy tale, the original version of *The Wonderful Wizard of Oz* was published in the year 1900. It was a big hit – its entire first printing sold out. The book has since been translated into more than 40 different languages and published across the world. A first-edition copy of the book once sold for more than $100,000!

There are 40 official sequels or prequels to *The Wonderful Wizard of Oz*, including 14 that were written by L. F. Baum, and 19 written by Ruth Plumly Thompson. But the original book, *The Wonderful Wizard of Oz*, is by far the most popular of all the *Oz* books.

The first musical version of *The Wonderful Wizard of Oz* was produced by Baum and Denslow in 1902. It used the same characters and had a long, successful run of nearly 300 shows from January 21, 1903, to December 31, 1904.

Silent film versions of *Oz* were made in 1910 and 1925. A seven-minute animated cartoon was made in 1933.

The first major film version of *Oz* was made by MGM and released in 1939 entitled *The Wizard of Oz*. It featured many musical numbers, including "Somewhere Over the Rainbow," which was chosen as the greatest movie song of all time by the American Film Institute in 2004. The movie also won several Academy Awards, including Best Picture, in the year of its release.

The Wizard of Oz movie only made a small profit upon its original release. However, the film was re-released in 1948 after the end of World War II to much greater success. But the film didn't begin to make a profit for MGM until after 1976!

The Wiz was a 1978 movie starring Diana Ross as Dorothy and Michael Jackson as the Scarecrow. It featured exclusively African-American actors.

The Wizard of Oz was made into a video game for the Super Nintendo gaming system in 1993. It was based on the 1939 film.

The Wizard of Oz on Ice was a touring production that performed across the world from 1995 to 1999.

Wicked is a 2003 musical based on the book *Wicked: The Life and Times of the Wicked Witch of the West* by Gregory Maguire. It tells the story of how the Wicked Witch of the West came to be so cruel. *Wicked* broke box office records in New York, Los Angeles, Chicago, St. Louis, and London.

ABOUT THE AUTHOR

LYMAN FRANK BAUM was an American author, poet, playwright, actor, and filmmaker. In 1900, Baum published *The Wonderful Wizard of Oz.* It is considered to be a classic of children's literature to this day. He has also written thirteen sequels to *Oz*, as well as a total of 55 novels, 82 short stories, more than 200 poems. He is considered by many to be a visionary, and had predicted that color TV and cell phones would be quite common in the near future.

ABOUT THE RETELLING AUTHOR

MARTIN POWELL has been a freelance writer since 1986. He has written hundreds of stories, many of which have been published by Disney, Marvel, Tekno Comix, Moonstone Books, and others. In 1989, Powell received an Eisner Award nomination for his graphic novel *Scarlet in Gaslight.* This award is one of the highest comic book honors.

ABOUT THE ILLUSTRATOR

JORGE BREAK was born in Mexico City, Mexico. At an early age, he developed a love of reading comic books and drawing. Jorge began working as a graphic designer and illustrator in 1993 and was published for the first time in *MAD Magazine* (Mexican Edition). Jorge has also illustrated for the Mexican Edition of Captain Tsubasa (a popular soccer Japanese-style manga), and from 2000 to 2007 he has worked on his own series, Meteorix 5.9. Stone Arch Books' adaptation of *The Wizard of Oz* is Jorge's first professional work published in the United States.

GLOSSARY

balloonist (buh-LOON-ist)—a person who pilots and maintains hot air balloons

bleak (BLEEK)—empty and depressing, or without hope

enchanted (en-CHAN-tid)—something that has been enchanted has been put under a magic spell or seems magical

ferocious (fuh-ROH-shuhss)—very fierce and savage

majesty (MAJ-uh-stee)—the formal title for a king or queen

meek (MEEK)—quiet, humble, and obedient

naive (nah-EEV)—not very experienced, or too trusting

poppies (POP-eez)—a poppy is a garden plant with large, red flowers

protect (pruh-TEKT)—guard or keep something safe from harm

sensitive (SEN-suh-tiv)—easily offended or hurt

spell (SPEL)—a word or words supposed to have magical powers

wicked (WIK-id)—very bad, cruel, or evil

wizard (WIZ-urd)—a person believed to have magic powers

DISCUSSION QUESTIONS

1. If you had a chance to ask the Wizard of Oz for one gift, what would it be? Would you ask for courage, like the lion, or something else? Explain your answer.

2. Why do you think Dorothy wanted to return home so badly? Would you have wanted to stay in the Land of Oz? Why or why not?

3. Have you seen or read other versions of *The Wizard of Oz*? If so, how were those versions different or the same than this story?

WRITING PROMPTS

1. What do you think happened to the other characters when Dorothy left the Emerald City? Choose a character and write about how they lived after Dorothy was gone.

2. The journey to the Emerald City was dangerous but also exciting. Write about the most exciting trip you've ever taken. Where did you go? What made the experience so memorable?

3. Dorothy's Silver Slippers had the power to take her home. If you had the power to be transported anywhere in the world, where would you go? Write about your choice and what you would do when you got there.

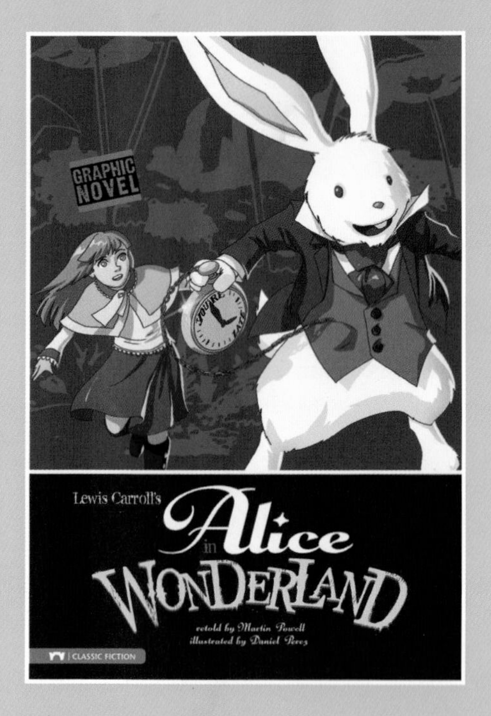

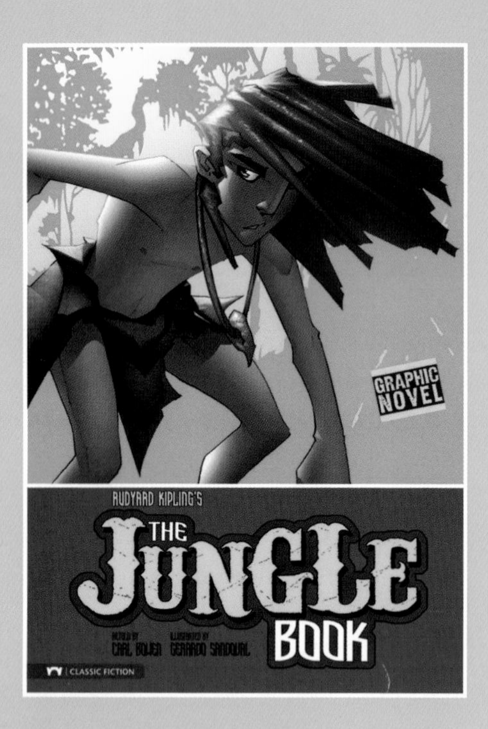

ALICE IN WONDERLAND

One day, a young girl named Alice spots a frantic White Rabbit wearing a waistcoat and carrying a pocket watch. She follows the hurried creature down a hole into the magical world of Wonderland. While there, Alice meets more crazy creatures, and plays a twisted game of croquet with the Queen of Hearts. But when the Queen turns against her, this dream-like world quickly becomes a nightmare.

THE JUNGLE BOOK

In the jungles of India, a pack of wolves discover a young boy. They name the boy Mowgli and protect him against dangers, including Shere Kan, the most savage tiger in the jungle. As Mowgli grows up, he learns the ways of the jungle from Bagheera the panther, the wise bear, Baloo, and other animals. Soon, he must decide whether to remain among beasts or embrace his own kind.

CLASSICS!

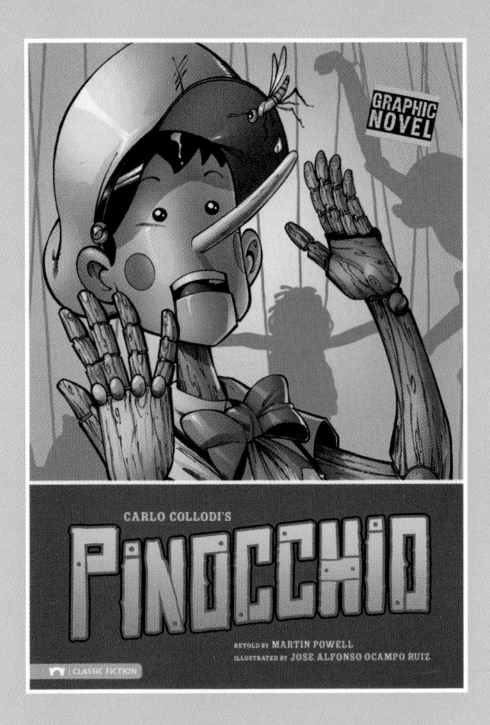

PINOCCHIO

Once upon a time, the dream of a lonely woodcutter is fulfilled when his puppet comes to life. Unfortunately, Pinocchio quickly becomes more of a prankster than a pleasure. He would rather create mischief and play tricks than keep up on his studies. Soon, however, the wooden puppet learns that being a real boy is much more complicated than simply having fun.

THE WIZARD OF OZ

On a bright summer day, a cyclone suddenly sweeps across the Kansas sky. A young girl named Dorothy and her dog, Toto, are carried up into the terrible storm. Far, far away, they crash down in a strange land called Oz. To return home, Dorothy must travel to the Emerald City and meet the all-powerful Wizard of Oz. But the journey won't be easy, and she'll need the help of a few good friends.